# CHASING THE TUNNELLING TRICKSTER

# DINOSAUR COVE

# DINOSAUR COVE™

## CHASING THE TUNNELLING TRICKSTER

by
REX STONE

Series created by
Working Partners Ltd

illustrated by
MIKE SPOOR

OXFORD
UNIVERSITY PRESS

Special thanks to Jan Burchett and Sara Vogler

For Liam Peter Dyche – First of a generation  R.S.

Dedicated to St Neot's Preparatory School and all those
artistic children, with thanks from Mike Spoor

## OXFORD
### UNIVERSITY PRESS

Great Clarendon Street, Oxford OX2 6DP
Oxford University Press is a department of the University of Oxford.
It furthers the University's objective of excellence in research, scholarship,
and education by publishing worldwide in

Oxford  New York

Auckland  Cape Town  Dar es Salaam  Hong Kong  Karachi
Kuala Lumpur  Madrid  Melbourne  Mexico City  Nairobi
New Delhi  Shanghai  Taipei  Toronto

With offices in

Argentina  Austria  Brazil  Chile  Czech Republic  France  Greece
Guatemala  Hungary  Italy  Japan  Poland  Portugal  Singapore
South Korea  Switzerland  Thailand  Turkey  Ukraine  Vietnam

Oxford is a registered trade mark of Oxford University Press
in the UK and in certain other countries

© Working Partners Limited 2010
Illustrations © Mike Spoor 2010
Eye logo © Dominic Harman 2010

Series created by Working Partners Ltd
Dinosaur Cove is a registered trademark of Working Partners Ltd

The moral rights of the author have been asserted

Database right Oxford University Press (maker)

First published 2010

British Library Cataloguing in Publication Data

Data available

ISBN: 978-0-19-272976-7

1 3 5 7 9 10 8 6 4 2

Printed in Great Britain by Cox and Wyman Ltd, Reading, Berkshire
Paper used in the production of this book is a natural,
recyclable product made from wood grown in sustainable forests
The manufacturing process conforms to the environmental
regulations of the country of origin

# FACT FILE

JAMIE MOVED FROM THE CITY TO LIVE IN THE LIGHTHOUSE AT DINOSAUR COVE. JAMIE'S DAD RUNS A DINOSAUR MUSEUM ON THE BOTTOM FLOOR OF THE LIGHTHOUSE. WHEN JAMIE GOES HUNTING FOR FOSSILS IN THE CRUMBLING CLIFFS ON THE BEACH HE MEETS A LOCAL BOY, TOM, AND THE TWO DISCOVER AN AMAZING SECRET: A WORLD WITH REAL, LIVE DINOSAURS! THE TRIASSIC AGE IS INCREDIBLE—AND THE BOYS COULD BE TRAPPED THERE FOREVER!

## JAMIE

- FULL NAME: JAMIE MORGAN
- AGE: 8 YEARS
- SIZE: 1 JATOM*
- TOP SPEED: 10 KPH
- LIKES: FOSSIL HUNTING AND LEARNING ABOUT DINOSAURS
- DISLIKES: BEING STUCK INDOORS

Jamie's eye

Jamie's foot

Jamie's hand

*NOTE: A JATOM IS THE SIZE OF JAMIE OR TOM: 125 CM TALL AND 27 KG IN WEIGHT

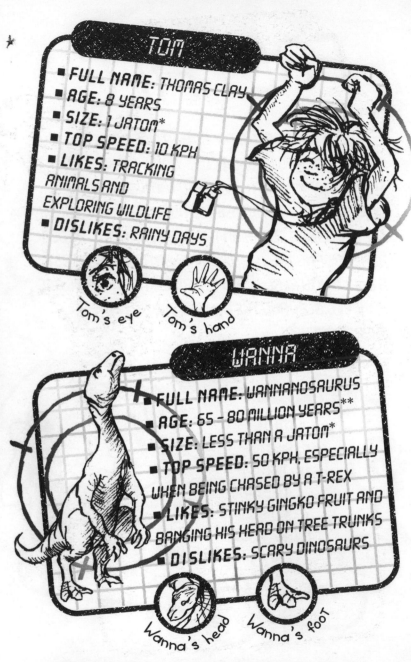

## TOM

- **FULL NAME:** THOMAS CLAY
- **AGE:** 8 YEARS
- **SIZE:** 1 JATOM*
- **TOP SPEED:** 10 KPH
- **LIKES:** TRACKING ANIMALS AND EXPLORING WILDLIFE
- **DISLIKES:** RAINY DAYS

Tom's eye    Tom's hand

## WANNA

- **FULL NAME:** WANNANOSAURUS
- **AGE:** 65 – 80 MILLION YEARS**
- **SIZE:** LESS THAN A JATOM*
- **TOP SPEED:** 50 KPH, ESPECIALLY WHEN BEING CHASED BY A T-REX
- **LIKES:** STINKY GINGKO FRUIT AND BANGING HIS HEAD ON TREE TRUNKS
- **DISLIKES:** SCARY DINOSAURS

Wanna's head    Wanna's foot

*NOTE: A JATOM IS THE SIZE OF JAMIE OR TOM: 125 CM TALL AND 27 KG IN WEIGHT
**NOTE: SCIENTISTS CALL THIS PERIOD THE LATE CRETACEOUS

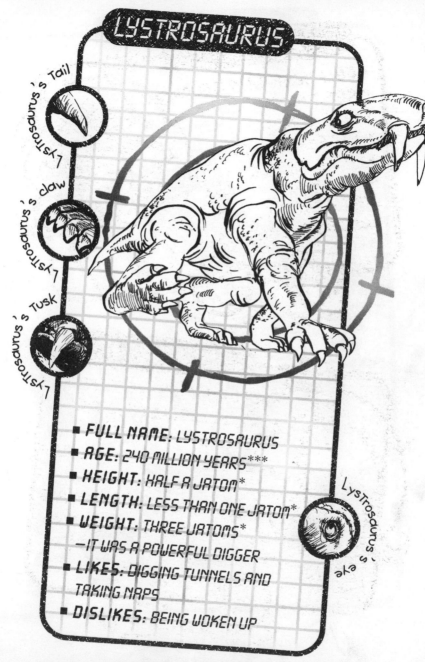

# LYSTROSAURUS

Lystrosaurus's Tail

Lystrosaurus's claw

Lystrosaurus's Tusk

Lystrosaurus's eye

- **FULL NAME:** LYSTROSAURUS
- **AGE:** 240 MILLION YEARS***
- **HEIGHT:** HALF A JATOM*
- **LENGTH:** LESS THAN ONE JATOM*
- **WEIGHT:** THREE JATOMS*
  —IT WAS A POWERFUL DIGGER
- **LIKES:** DIGGING TUNNELS AND TAKING NAPS
- **DISLIKES:** BEING WOKEN UP

*NOTE: A JATOM IS THE SIZE OF JAMIE OR TOM: 125 CM TALL AND 27 KG IN WEIGHT
***NOTE: SCIENTISTS CALL THIS PERIOD THE TRIASSIC

DINOSAUR COVE

Village

Marina

Sealight Head

# CHAPTER 1

'Awesome!' exclaimed Jamie Morgan to his best friend, Tom Clay.

He was standing in front of the new Time Tunnel that led from the cliff path to the main entrance of his dad's dinosaur museum. Mr Morgan had been working on the long, arched tunnel all week, and now it was finished. It looked as if it was made of solid rock.

'It looks so cool.' Tom knocked on the wall. 'Who'd think it was fibreglass?'

'We're the first to go in,' said Jamie in delight, as they stepped through the open mouth of a model T-Rex and into the sudden dark.

They were bathed in green light and a recorded voice echoed round them. **'Get ready to journey back millions of years in time—to the age of the dinosaurs.'**

Jamie and Tom grinned at each other. This tunnel might pretend to be going back in time, but they'd done it for real! Deep in the cliffs of Dinosaur Cove they'd discovered a secret world. A land of living dinosaurs!

As they moved on, images of prehistoric creatures appeared on screens. Deep rumbling growls surrounded them.

**'You are now in the Cretaceous Age,'** announced the voice, **'sixty-five million years ago.'**

'Wow!' said Jamie. 'Look at those velociraptors . . . and the ankylosaurus.'

ENTRANCE

'Just like we remember them,' said Tom.
As they walked on the light turned
yellow. **'Prepare to go back even further in
time,'** boomed the voice. **'To the Jurassic,
one hundred and fifty
million years
ago.'**

TRIASSIC

Jamie
pointed at the
next screen. 'There's
a stegosaurus.'

'And here's a plesiosaur,' added
Tom. 'We've seen one of those up close.'

'Too close!' laughed Jamie. 'I'll never
forget those teeth.'

They moved on and the light turned
orange.

'And now we've arrived at the end of our
journey—the Triassic Age,' the voice went

on. **'Over two hundred million years ago. The Dawn of the Dinosaurs.'**

'We've never been as far back as this,' said Jamie, examining the screens. 'I don't recognize any of these dinos.'

'We don't know much about the Triassic,' said Tom.

'Let's check out what Dad's got on display,' suggested Jamie.

They stepped out of the tunnel into the museum at the bottom of Jamie's lighthouse home. They raced round the table with its Cretaceous landscape, under the edmontosaurus skeleton, and past the triceratops skull.

'I can't find anything from the Triassic. There's nothing older than two hundred million years!' said Jamie.

'We'd better ask your dad,' said Tom.

They found Mr Morgan arranging a shelf of Jurassic teeth.

'Hello, boys,' he said. 'What do you think of my Time Tunnel?'

'It's cool, Dad,' said Jamie. 'Almost like really going back in time.'

Tom coughed to hide a laugh. 'We were wondering if there are any Triassic dinos here?' he asked. 'Like the pictures in the tunnel.'

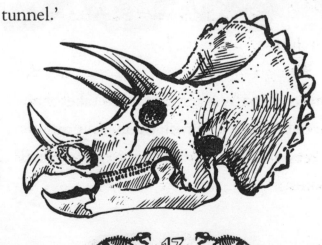

'Not at the moment,' said Mr Morgan. 'But that's my next job now the tunnel's finished.'

'We'll do some research for you,' said Jamie with a wink at Tom.

They headed off to the 'Keys of the Past' exhibit, where a glass case mounted on the wall held a display of ammonites. Below was a sand pit with plastic trowels where kids could dig up fossils and use the labelled exhibits in the case to identify them. Whenever the boys

Permian        Triassic        Jurassic        Cretaceous

went to Dino World they had to take the right ammonite with them, as it was their own secret key to the age they wanted to visit.

They climbed into the sand pit.

'That's what we need,' exclaimed Jamie, pointing. 'That rough-looking one labelled "Triassic".'

The boys delved in the sand.

Jamie unearthed an ammonite. 'Too round,' said Jamie. He dug again. 'No, too smooth . . . How about this?'

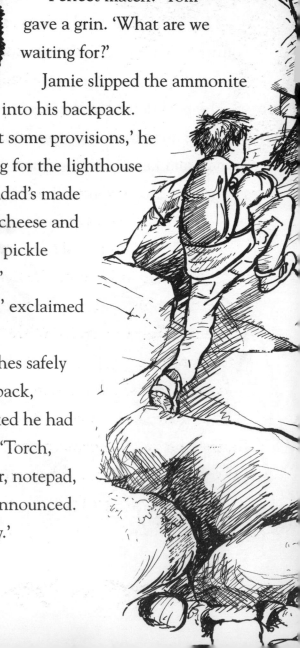

'Perfect match!' Tom gave a grin. 'What are we waiting for?'

Jamie slipped the ammonite into his backpack.

'Let's get some provisions,' he said, heading for the lighthouse stairs. 'Grandad's made some of his cheese and home-made pickle sandwiches.'

'Yummy!' exclaimed Tom.

Sandwiches safely in the backpack, Jamie checked he had everything. 'Torch, Fossil Finder, notepad, lunch,' he announced. 'We're ready.'

They bounded
down the steps and
across the sand. Soon
they were hauling
themselves up the
boulders of Smuggler's
Point to where their secret
world was hidden, deep in
an old cave.

Jamie could feel excitement
bubbling inside him like fizzy lemonade
as he shone his torch on the five fossilized
dinosaur footprints that led to the back wall
of the dark cave.

He took out the ammonite.

'OK, little fossil. Time to take us to the
Triassic,' he said. He glanced back at Tom.
'Do you think Wanna will be waiting for us?'

'The sooner we get there the sooner we'll
know,' said Tom.

Wanna was a little Cretaceous dinosaur, a wannanosaurus who went with them on all their adventures. Jamie stepped into the first print. 'One . . . two . . .' he counted. Tom was close behind. 'Three . . . four . . . **five** . . .'

There was a flash, the wall disappeared, and the hard footprints beneath their feet turned to soft mud. The boys found themselves in the hollowed out trunk of a rotting tree, swarming with beetles.

'Cool!' said Jamie. 'Look at the size of them.'

They stepped out, their feet crunching on dried pine needles.

'Triassic or not, this is definitely different from anything we've seen before!' exclaimed Tom, gazing at their new surroundings.

'It's just as hot as the Jurassic and Cretaceous times,' said Jamie. 'But not as damp.'

'There aren't so many trees,' said Tom. 'And they're smaller.'

The air was full of croaks and strange rattling cries. Moth-like flies flew over their heads.

'But are we in the Triassic?' Jamie
wondered. 'The ammonite might have been
wrongly labelled.'

'We need firm evidence,' said Tom.

A small, brightly coloured lizard suddenly
leapt off one of the trees and glided to the

ground on leathery
wings, where it
gobbled up a beetle.

'A gliding lizard!'
gasped Tom. 'Look it up.'

Jamie got out his Fossil
Finder, the clever handheld
computer that was full of dino facts. Up came
the *HAPPY HUNTING* screen. He typed in the
keywords—*GLIDING LIZARD, ROUNDED WING TIPS,
INSECT EATER*—and pressed 'enter'.

'*ICAROSAURUS*,' he read from the screen.
'*LIZARD ABLE TO GLIDE SHORT DISTANCES USING
RIBBED SKIN BETWEEN ITS FRONT AND BACK LEGS.
LIVED IN THE TRIASSIC AGE!*'

'That proves it,' said Tom. 'We've made it
back to the Dawn of the Dinosaurs!'

'Cool!' said Jamie as they high-fived. Then
he frowned. '*We've* made it back—but where's
Wanna?'

'Wanna!' Jamie called. 'Where are you?'
Exploring this new world wouldn't be as much
fun without their friend.

The boys heard a trampling sound from
the undergrowth.

'Wanna!' called Tom. 'We're over here.'

But it wasn't Wanna.

'Look out!' Jamie yelled. He grabbed Tom
and dragged him behind a tree just as a troop
of small, skinny dinosaurs rushed by.

'Thanks!' Tom grinned at his friend.

'I've seen those creatures in a
book,' said Jamie. 'They're
eoraptors. Cool! Our first real-
live Triassic dinosaur.'

But Tom's grin had vanished.
'There's no sign of Wanna.
Maybe he can't go this far back
in time.'

*Grunk!* A small sturdy shape burst
through the bushes with half a sloppy
orange gingko fruit in its mouth.
It bounded round the boys like
a puppy, giving them
sandpapery licks.

'Get off, Wanna!' laughed Jamie, rubbing
the pulp off his clothes.

'Phwoar!' exclaimed Tom, holding his nose.

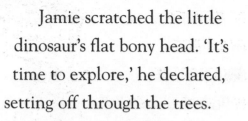

Jamie scratched the little dinosaur's flat bony head. 'It's time to explore,' he declared, setting off through the trees.

'Let's see how different the Triassic world is.'

They set off past a large pond. They hadn't gone very far when Tom stopped and bent down, hands on his knees. 'Strange,' he said. 'I'm puffed out, and we've only been walking.' He looked up at Jamie. 'Your cheeks are all red.'

Jamie's heart was racing and he was finding it difficult to take deep breaths.

'I feel like I've run a marathon,' he said, dropping to his knees on the ground. He pulled out his Fossil Finder and punched some keys. '*THE TRIASSIC AIR CONTAINED MUCH LESS OXYGEN*,' he read. '*THIS MAY HAVE BEEN A CAUSE*

*OF THE MASS EXTINCTION OF LIFE AT THE BEGINNING OF THIS PERIOD—'*

THE TRIASSIC AIR CONTAINED MUCH LESS OXYGEN

SEARCH: TRIASSIC

'*—WHEN NINETY-FIVE PER CENT OF LIFE WAS WIPED OUT!*' Tom read over his shoulder.

'Wow! We'd better take it slowly if we don't want to be wiped out too.'

Wanna walked on ahead, panting hard. The boys followed, stepping out into the scorching sunshine of a dried-up river bank. Jagged cracks ran across the baked earth under their feet.

A thin trickle of brown muddy water wormed past them. Tom splashed his hands in the flow. 'Even this stream's hot,' he said.

Wanna trotted over to it and took great
gulps of water.

'Wish we could do that,' said Jamie,
wiping his brow. 'But I don't think it would
taste too good.'

 32

'We need to start a map of our latest Dino World,' said Tom. 'Look, there's a tree over there, and a log to sit on. We'll be out of the sun and still have a great view of the area.'

They splashed their way to the log through shallow puddles where steam was rising in the heat. The trickle of water had thinned to almost nothing.

'This is all that's left of the river,' said Tom. 'We must be in the dry season.'

They reached the log and flopped down on it. Jamie took out his notebook, in which they'd made maps of their previous worlds, and turned to a new page. He began to sketch the rotten tree, the pond, and the route of the dried-up river. 'I'll put in what we know of the stream,' he said, 'although I can't tell where it comes from. And those hills in the distance.'

'It'll be easy to mark the trees,' said Tom. 'There are hardly any. And no grass at all.'

 33

Wanna settled in the shade beside them, tongue hanging out.

'That's odd,' said Tom. 'Look at those funny mounds over there.'

Jamie glanced over at the tall round piles of fresh, loose earth near the riverbed. In the centre of each one was a deep hole. 'They remind me of molehills,' he exclaimed.

'Made by huge dino moles,' said Tom, grinning.

An echoing *honk* suddenly came from one of the holes.

The boys looked at each other. 'What's that?' said Jamie.

Wanna was listening hard, his head on one side.

Then came another *honk*—from the hole nearest the boys.

'Something's moving underground,' said Tom. 'And it's coming towards us!'

The ground in front of the boys began to heave.

'Hide!' yelled Tom.

Jamie stuffed his map and pencil into his backpack and the boys scrambled down behind the log with Wanna. Now earth was shooting into the air.

A horny beak appeared, sniffed the air and pushed upwards. Two wide, clawed feet followed, and a creature about the size of a pig heaved itself slowly out of the ground. It shook the dust

from its bony head, ambled off on four stout legs and started munching a solitary fern.

'Check out those tusks!' whispered Jamie. 'Looks like it's been in a fight. One of them is broken.'

'They point downwards like fangs,' laughed Tom. 'It's a Triassic Dracula!'

'I don't think it's going to sink them into us though,' said Jamie. 'It doesn't look like a meat-eating dinosaur—in fact I'm not sure it's a dinosaur at all.' He rummaged for his Fossil Finder.

Tom turned to an imaginary camera. 'Tom Clay reporting from the Triassic age, where our intrepid explorers are facing their first prehistoric puzzle. What sort of creature is Broken-Tusk?'

 39

Jamie tapped a description of the creature into the Fossil Finder.

'Our mystery beast's about a metre long,' Tom went on, 'with beady eyes, a bony ridge on its head, a beak like a turtle's, and fangs. Let's hear what Professor Morgan has to say . . . Over to you, professor.'

Jamie scanned the information on the Fossil Finder screen. 'Well, viewers, Broken-Tusk is a lystrosaurus,' he announced. 'The name means "shovel lizard", because it has short broad hands for digging.' He scrolled down. 'It's a herbivore. And guess what—I was right. It's not a dinosaur!'

'What is it then?' asked Tom.

'A mammal-like reptile,' Jamie read. 'They're one of the few who survived the big extinction at the beginning of the Triassic.'

'Good for them!' declared Tom. 'Go, lystros!'

40

'But they only lasted about twenty million years,' added Jamie. 'They were slow and had no defences, so they made a nice easy meal when the big dinosaurs came along.'

They watched the lystrosaurus tear at the fern with its tusks.

*Splitch!* Something plopped into one of the nearby puddles. Wanna poked his nose into the water and jumped back in surprise. The boys went over to take a look.

Two bulbous eyes stared up at them from the puddle. Suddenly the water rippled and a small yellow and green creature with a pink

belly sprang out. It hopped past them on
webbed feet.

'A Triassic frog!' exclaimed Jamie.
'Awesome colours!' He made for the log again
to pick up his things. 'Let's
explore the—' He
broke off and his
jaw dropped
open.

'What's up?'
asked Tom. 'You
look like a gawping
goldfish.'

'The backpack!' gasped Jamie,
searching round the log. 'It's gone.'

'It can't have,' said Tom. Jamie watched as

he scanned the area and burst out laughing. 'It looks like Broken-Tusk has run off with it. I bet it smelt your grandad's pickle and wants to get a taste.'

But Jamie wasn't laughing. 'Have you forgotten?' he gulped. 'The ammonite's in there!'

'Our key to the Triassic age,' said Tom, his face turning pale.

'And our key home.' Jamie felt a tingle of fear run down his spine. 'We could be stuck in Dino World for ever!'

43

Jamie and Tom dashed after the lystrosaurus, Wanna at their heels. But the cheeky lystro vanished down one of its holes.

Falling to his knees Tom put his ear to the hole. 'I can't hear it,' he said. 'It must have gone down one of the tunnels.'

'It could be anywhere by now!' groaned Jamie.

Something honked loudly behind them. They spun round to see a lystro sticking its horny beak up from the ground.

*Onk!*

'That's not our thief,' said Jamie, disappointed. 'We're after Broken-Tusk, and that one's tusks are intact.'

The lystro stared solemnly at them and then let out a loud *Onk!*

Immediately answering calls filled the air around them and lystros began popping up out of the holes.

'I think it's told its friends to come and look at the strange two-legged creatures,' said Tom.

*Onk!*

*Onk!*

*Onk!*

'It's doing our job for us,' said Jamie. 'Now we can check their tusks.'

The boys darted from one hole to the next. Wanna charged along at their side.

'This is turning into a whack-a-mole game!' panted Jamie. 'And we're getting nowhere. Our lystro's not appearing.' He was sweating hard now.

Tom stopped to catch his breath. 'I've got an idea. We lure it out.'

'Brilliant,' grinned Jamie. 'But how?'

Tom pointed at the forest. 'We get some gingkoes and dangle them down the holes on the ends of vines. The smell should be enough to bring Broken-Tusk running.'

'Awesome,' said Jamie. 'Triassic fishing!'

They ran to the nearest gingko tree. Tom tore off a length of vine that twisted round the trunk. Then the boys picked the smelly orange fruit, holding them in the front of their T-shirts.

*Grunk!* Wanna ran around between them.

'He thinks it's dinner time!' laughed Jamie.

'Sorry, boy,' said Tom. 'We need these.'

They ran back to the dried riverbed.

'Broken-Tusk disappeared somewhere here,' said Tom, catching his breath.

'Then this hole will be as good as any,'

declared Jamie, tying the
vine round a gingko and
lowering it down.

*Grunk!* No sooner had
the gingko disappeared
than Wanna dived in after
it. The boys heard a loud
slurping noise.

'No, Wanna!' cried
Jamie, whipping the
vine back. It was
empty. 'He's
guzzled the
whole thing.'

'Try again,' said Tom.

Jamie peered down the hole. 'Won't work. He's waiting. I could try another hole.' He tiptoed over to the next mound. 'It's no good. I can hear him coming!'

Grunk! Wanna's happy cry echoed up.

'Broken-Tusk's not going to come near while Wanna's there,' said Tom.

'Then we'll have to get him out,' said Jamie. He looked down the hole and waved a gingko at the little dinosaur. 'Here, boy!'

But Wanna spun round and scampered out of sight, exploring further down the tunnel.

'Where's he gone?' asked Tom.

With a shower of stones Wanna appeared from a nearby hole. He jumped out and ran between the mounds, stopping at each one and sniffing hard.

All of a sudden he froze, head on one side.

*Grunk! Grunk!* Wanna looked at them eagerly and pawed the mound.

'I think he's calling us over,' said Tom.

They darted towards him.

'Did you hear that?' hissed Jamie. 'A sort of snaffling noise.'

A deafening squeal hit their ears.

'SQQQUUEEAAAAGGGHHHH!'

'Something sounds angry,' said Tom.

'Too right!' yelled Jamie.

'And it's coming up!'

CHAPTER 5

A lystrosaurus burst out of the hole. Head down, it charged towards the nearest puddle, tossing Wanna into the air as it went. It plunged its head into the water, sucking it up with loud gulps.

'Look at its right tusk,' said Jamie. 'It's broken. Wanna's found our thief. Well done, boy.'

'And there's bread hanging from its mouth,' laughed Tom. 'It's been eating our sandwiches.'

'Grandad's homemade pickle must have been too hot for Broken-Tusk!' grinned Jamie.

Tom peered down into the hole. 'No sign of the backpack. Broken-Tusk must have left it down there.'

'We'll have to go into the tunnels,' said Jamie.

'Yahoo!' yelled Tom as he slid feet first into the gloomy hole and disappeared from sight.

Jamie sat on the edge of the mound and pushed off.

'Whee!' he cried as he slithered down the slope and crashed into Tom. A low, wide burrow stretched out in front of them.

'We'll have to crawl from here,' said Tom. 'This tunnel's lystro size.'

The boys scrambled along on all fours. It was very gloomy in the tunnel but every

now and then a trickle of daylight filtered down from one of the holes. Wanna padded along behind them.

'Phwoar!' gasped Jamie, waving a hand in front of his nose. 'This place could do with a fan.'

'It's difficult to breathe,' panted Tom. 'The air smells really stale.'

'Maybe that's why the lystrosaurs survived into the Triassic age,' said Jamie. 'When the air got thinner and killed off most of the other creatures the lystros were already used to it because they lived in such stuffy tunnels.'

'Brilliant deduction!' said Tom. 'Tell your dad that theory when we get back.'

Jamie peered ahead. On the floor where the tunnel forked, he could see something. It looked like a loop of blue fabric.

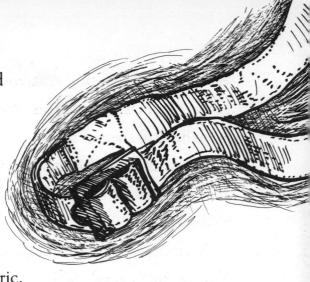

'It's the strap of the backpack!' he cried. The strap vanished round the corner.

'A lystro must have it,' yelled Tom.

Scrambling along on their hands and knees, the boys chased the backpack with its precious ammonite. Wanna hurried along behind, grunking happily as if it was a game.

With each twist and turn of the tunnels,

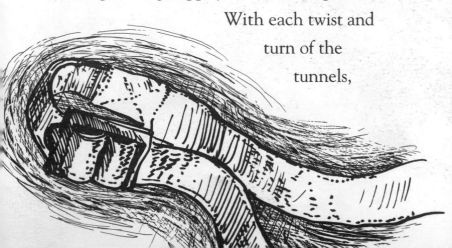

they'd catch sight of a flash of blue backpack
before it was whisked away again. Jamie
turned a corner, just ahead of Tom.

'Oh no!' he exclaimed.

Tom joined him and the boys stared
in dismay.

Further down the tunnel,
a lystrosaurus with

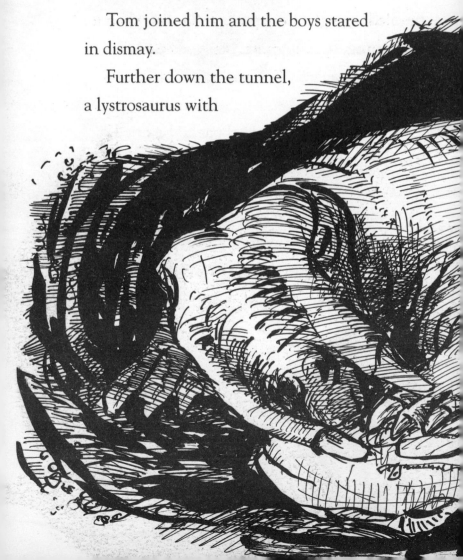

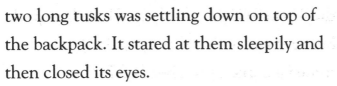

two long tusks was settling down on top of
the backpack. It stared at them sleepily and
then closed its eyes.

'We'll soon shift it,' muttered Tom. He
pulled a gingko from pocket. 'Jamie, when it
wakes up, you snatch the backpack.'

The boys crawled along
the tunnel.

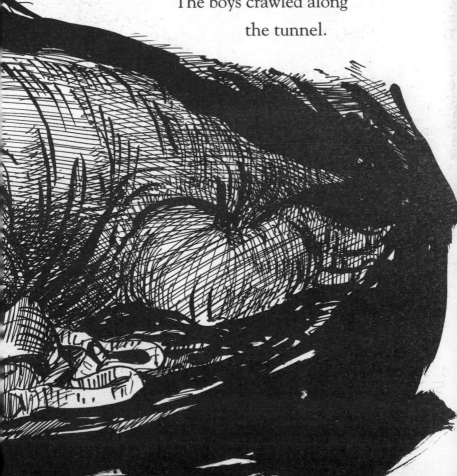

Tom tapped the lystro on the snout. One scaly
eyelid opened.

'Up you get,' called Tom.

*Honk!* The lystrosaurus opened both eyes
and sniffed the air.

'Time for a snack,' said
Tom, waving the gingko in front
of its snout.

The lystro gave an angry snort and got to
its feet.

'Uh oh!' he whispered. 'It doesn't look happy.'

'Maybe waking it up wasn't such a good idea,' muttered Jamie.

The creature shook its bony head from side to side. Suddenly it opened its mouth wide and lurched forwards.

# CHAPTER 6

SEARCH:

'Look out!' yelled Jamie, dragging Tom back down the tunnel.

The lystro put its head down and charged.

Jamie and Tom cowered against the wall, covering their heads, and Wanna scampered back in fright as the thundering of the lystro's feet got closer.

Then it all went quiet. Jamie and Tom peered through their fingers. The lystro had come to a stop. It gave a yawn, filling the tunnel with its hot stinky breath.

Then it lumbered away and flopped onto the backpack again.

'I'm glad you're too lazy to chase us away, Mr Lystro,' chuckled Tom.

'But what do we do?' groaned Jamie.

There was a scuffling noise from behind. Wanna was backing away down the tunnel, a determined look on his face.

'He looks as if he's revving up,' said Jamie.

*Grunk!* Wanna was suddenly galloping forwards. He barged between them, throwing their bodies against the walls.

'He's charging the lystro,' gasped Tom.

'No, Wanna!' yelled Jamie. 'You'll get hurt!'

Head down, Wanna rocketed into the lystro's bottom! WHACK!

The creature woke and struggled to its feet, its head shaking from side to side. Then it saw Wanna. It sounded a long, deep snort. Wanna gave a warning grunk in reply.

'Here, Wanna!' Jamie called. 'Come away, boy.'

*Honk!* The stocky creature turned round to face Wanna. It took a step towards him.

*GRUNK!* Wanna was not going to be beaten. He began to paw the ground. The

lystro raised its head as if it was going to gouge him with its tusks.

Jamie and Tom were about to scramble to Wanna's rescue when the lystrosaurus gave a disgruntled honk and shuffled away. Wanna snatched up the squashed backpack.

'Well done, Wanna! You brave boy,' cried Jamie, taking the rucksack from him. 'We can get home!'

'As long as the ammonite's still in there,' said Tom grimly.

Jamie looked at him. 'If it dropped out somewhere in these tunnels we'll never find it!' Heart pounding, he tugged open the backpack and plunged a hand inside. 'Notebook . . . pencils . . . and what's this?'

He pulled out a half-chewed cheese and pickle sandwich.

'Yuck!' exclaimed Tom.

Then Jamie's fingers closed round

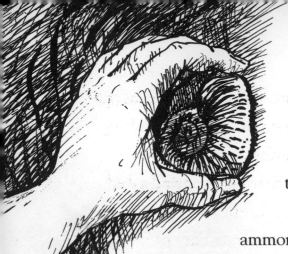

something cold
and hard. He
held it up in
triumph.

'The
ammonite!' gasped
Tom. 'We can go home. All
thanks to you, Wanna.' He patted
the little dinosaur on the head.

'But where are we?' said Jamie. 'It's a maze
down here.'

'No problem.' Tom was grinning. 'We just
pop up the nearest hole—like a lystro.'

They followed the tunnel to the next
glimmer of light and clawed their way up the
steep hole, Wanna scrambling behind.

They climbed out and Tom took a deep
breath. 'There might not be a lot of air up
here but it's a lot easier to breathe than
underground—as long as we take it slowly.'

'Let's just stick to the Time Tunnel at the museum from now on,' said Jamie, brushing the earth off his clothes.

'Remember our first Jurassic trip?' asked Tom as they headed for the hollow tree. 'We were scared Wanna wouldn't be able to go back to his Cretaceous time.'

Jamie nodded. 'Little did
we know how magic he is!'
They reached the hollowed out
tree. Wanna gave a goodbye grunk,
charged right into the middle of it
and disappeared with a FLASH!
'Our turn now,' declared Tom.
The boys put their feet into
Wanna's muddy footprints and
walked backwards into the
hollow tree. There was
an even bigger
FLASH!

and they found themselves back in the old
smugglers' cave.

Dad was about to put up the closed sign on
the museum's door when they burst in.

'We saw . . . I mean we found out loads
about lystrosaurs today,' said Jamie.

'Lystrosaurs,' said Mr Morgan thoughtfully. 'They survived the mass extinction at the beginning of the Triassic, didn't they?'

'Jamie has a theory about that,' said Tom.

'It might be because they were tunnellers and used to living in stale air,' Jamie told his dad. 'The Triassic air was really thin—not much oxygen.'

'Don't we know it!' muttered Tom.

'Clever idea, son,' said Mr Morgan. 'You could be right.'

'Shame we haven't got much about the Triassic here,' said Jamie. 'It's different from when the huge dinos ruled the earth,

 74

but just as exciting. What if Tom and I build our own exhibit?'

'That's a cool idea!' exclaimed Tom.

Mr Morgan grinned. 'I'll get you a table.' He went off to find one.

'We'll have a model of that gliding icarosaurus,' said Jamie, eyes shining, 'and some eoraptors.'

'There are those dino frogs too,' put in Tom.

'Don't forget the lystro,' Jamie said. 'But no backpack,' he added with a smile.

'I've got the perfect name for our new display,' declared Tom. 'The Dawn of the Dinosaurs!'

# GLOSSARY

**Cretaceous (cret-ay-shus)** – from about 65 to 150 million years ago, this time period was home to the widest variety of dinosaur and insect life of any period. Birds replaced winged dinosaurs, while in the sea, sharks and rays multiplied.

**Eoraptor (ee-oh-rap-tor)** – a small, lightly built dinosaur with hollow bones, much like today's birds. It stood on two legs and was a speedy runner, using its clawed arms to grasp its prey of lizards and worms.

**Gingko (gink-oh)** – a tree native to China called a 'living fossil' because fossils of it have been found dating back millions of years, yet they are still around today. Also known as the stink bomb tree because of its smelly apricot-like fruit.

**Icarosaurus (ick-ar-ro-sor-us)** – a tiny, thin dinosaur with four legs and a tail the length of its body. It had a set of long ribs covered with skin that formed wings, allowing it to glide.

**Jurassic (jur-as-sick)** – from about 150 to 200 million years ago, the Jurassic age was warm and humid, with lush jungle cover and great marine diversity. Large dinosaurs ruled on land, while the first birds took to the air.

**Lystrosaurus (list-ro-sor-us)** – a heavily built herbivore about the size of a pig. It walked on all fours, nesting in burrows dug out with its powerful front legs. Instead of teeth it had two tusks.

**Triassic (try-as-sick)** – from about 200 to 250 million years ago, during this time period seed plants and spiney trees flourished on land along with many species of reptiles and, eventually, the first dinosaurs.

**Wannanosaurus (wah-nan-oh-sor-us)** – a dinosaur that only ate plants and used its hard, flat skull to defend itself. Named after the place it was discovered: Wannano in China.

# Snap! Snap!
## Watch out for our teeth!

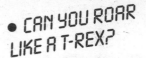